The Wishing Chair

The *Wishing* *Chair*

by Rick Dupré

Carolrhoda Books, Inc.
Minneapolis

It was a sunny July Sunday. The
cement of Granny Thelma's steps
was hot to the touch, and the smell
of her peonies was sweet in the heavy
summer air.

As usual, Eldon was spending his Sunday
playing at Granny Thelma's while his mom
was off at work in the city. Eldon loved to sit
on the steps and watch people as they walked
by. Almost everyone had a smile or a
wave for Thelma's Sunday guest.

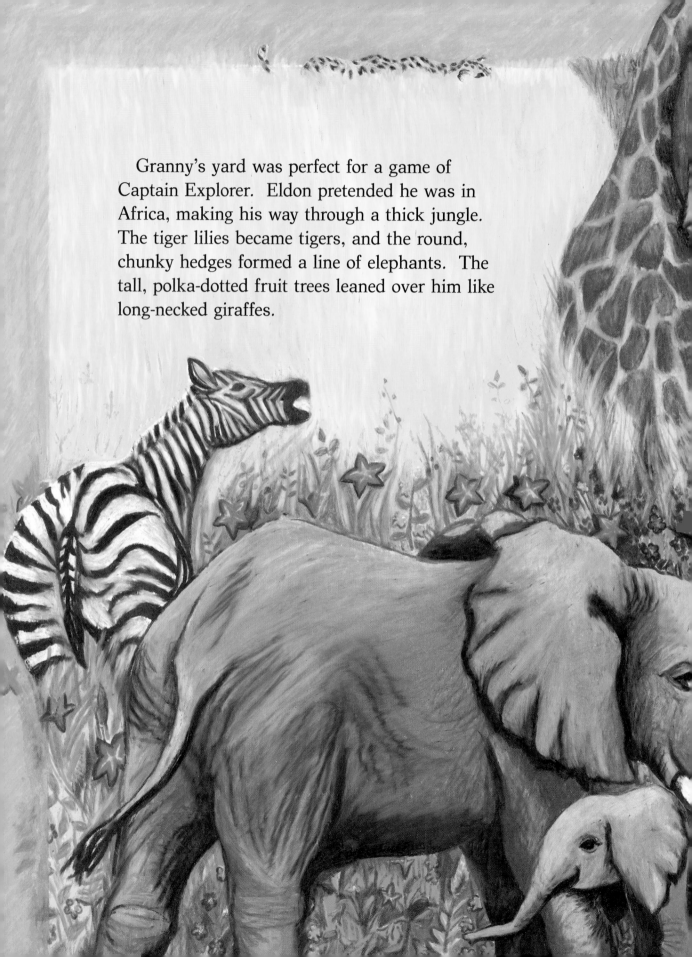

Granny's yard was perfect for a game of Captain Explorer. Eldon pretended he was in Africa, making his way through a thick jungle. The tiger lilies became tigers, and the round, chunky hedges formed a line of elephants. The tall, polka-dotted fruit trees leaned over him like long-necked giraffes.

Of course, some days the jungle was a bit too wet or a bit too cold, and Eldon would have to play inside. This was by no means second-best, because the house held plenty of adventures.

While Granny worked in the big room, Eldon would play all around, in little rooms with slanting ceilings and in warm rooms with soft carpet floors. Sometimes Eldon played that the house was a ship, and he would stumble around with the tossing of the waves.

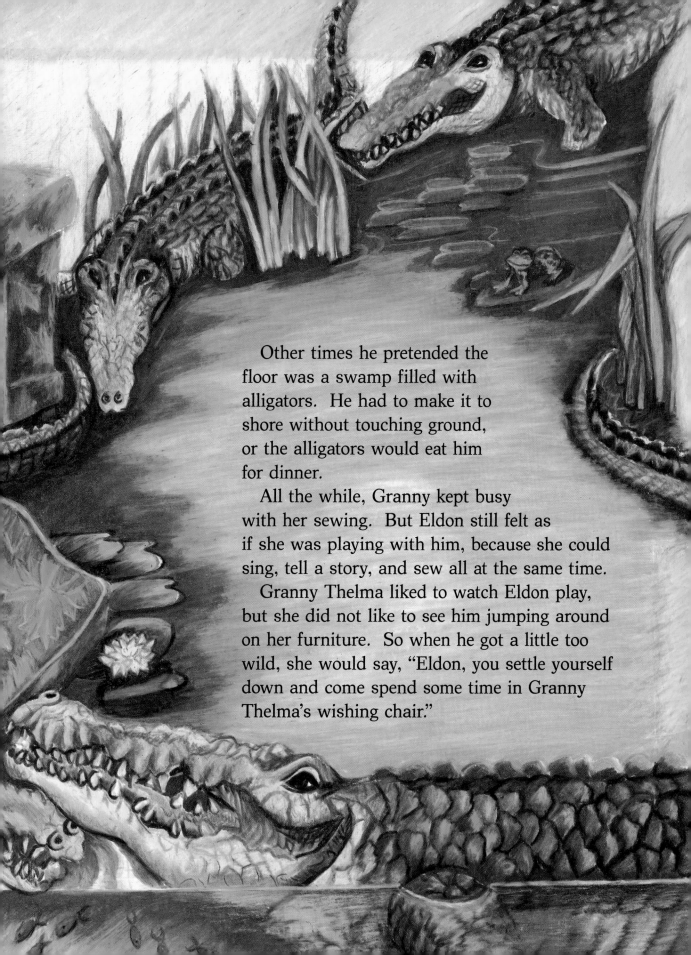

Other times he pretended the
floor was a swamp filled with
alligators. He had to make it to
shore without touching ground,
or the alligators would eat him
for dinner.

All the while, Granny kept busy
with her sewing. But Eldon still felt as
if she was playing with him, because she could
sing, tell a story, and sew all at the same time.

Granny Thelma liked to watch Eldon play,
but she did not like to see him jumping around
on her furniture. So when he got a little too
wild, she would say, "Eldon, you settle yourself
down and come spend some time in Granny
Thelma's wishing chair."

It was a big old chair, particularly comfortable for upside-down sitting and exactly the right size for Eldon to take a warm, curled-in-a-ball Sunday afternoon nap. Above the chair hung pictures of important people. Thelma said they were "the people who helped her wake up each morning and the people she said thank you to each night."

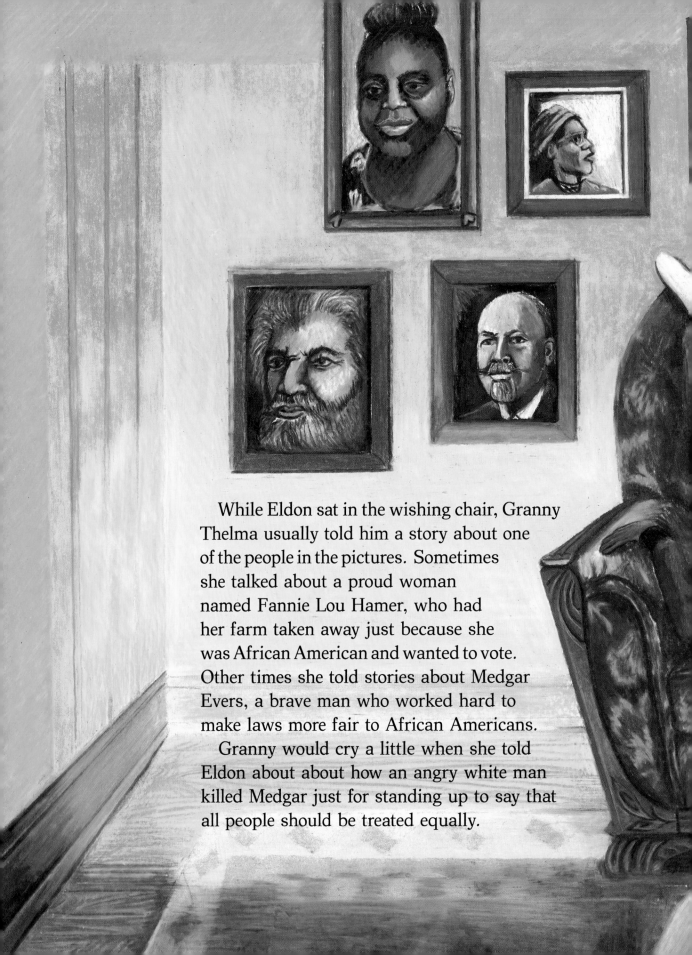

While Eldon sat in the wishing chair, Granny
Thelma usually told him a story about one
of the people in the pictures. Sometimes
she talked about a proud woman
named Fannie Lou Hamer, who had
her farm taken away just because she
was African American and wanted to vote.
Other times she told stories about Medgar
Evers, a brave man who worked hard to
make laws more fair to African Americans.

Granny would cry a little when she told
Eldon about about how an angry white man
killed Medgar just for standing up to say that
all people should be treated equally.

Eldon loved to listen to Granny's stories. He imagined that he was handsome and brave like Martin Luther King, Jr. He would make great speeches, and people would cheer. Or he pictured himself as a teacher like Septima Clark, helping other African Americans learn to read. And sometimes he tried to put words together like Langston Hughes. Perhaps someday he too could write poems that his people would be proud of and that everyone would love to read.

All of Eldon's daydreams were wonderful, but there was something else he liked to do in the wishing chair too, and that was wish. He wished he were taller so his legs could reach the pedals on his brother's bike. He wished his dog, Fella, were really a lion so he could ride him through his jungle. He wished he had enough money so that his mom did not have to work on Sundays.

But, when Eldon stood before the mark on the wall and saw he had not grown an inch, and Fella just lay down when Eldon tried to ride him, and his mom went to work as usual, Eldon doubted that the wishing chair had any power at all. So Eldon would ask his granny, "Why do you call this the wishing chair if it doesn't make wishes come true?"

Granny would always answer, "You start wishing for the right things, and they'll start coming true." Eldon didn't understand what that meant. All he knew was, if it didn't make his wishes come true, then it wasn't a very good wishing chair. But he still made wishes anyway, just in case.

As Eldon grew older, his games and wishes changed. Bicycle wishes turned into motorbike wishes. Jungle games gave way to dreams of flying to real jungles in faraway countries like Kenya and Ghana. But no matter what his age, Eldon never tired of one pastime: listening to Granny Thelma's stories.

Eventually Eldon was old enough to take care of himself on Sundays, but he always knew he could call on Granny Thelma if he had any trouble.

On days when Eldon needed a little extra help with his schoolwork, he would stop by to see Granny. If he couldn't decide what to get his mom for her birthday, Thelma always had a great idea.

Sometimes he stopped by just because he was lonesome.

During one of these visits, Thelma shared some sad news with Eldon. She explained that she was growing tired of the long, cold Minnesota winters, and she missed Mississippi, the state where she had grown up. She was ready for warm southern breezes and cold lemonade and the sight of her sister Mattie's smiling face. Thelma had decided to move back home. Eldon helped her pack.

Eldon wrapped dishes in paper and packed up
teapots and old clocks. He carried out box after box
marked "kitchen," "fragile," and "sentimental."
He loaded dressers and chairs and tables and
lamps. He rolled up rugs and lingered over old
photographs.

Granny's little house was overflowing with
wonderful memories. The old wardrobe, with its
dark wood and dusty smell, had been the perfect
hiding place. The well-worn cushions from
Granny's green couch had been islands in
his alligator-filled lake.

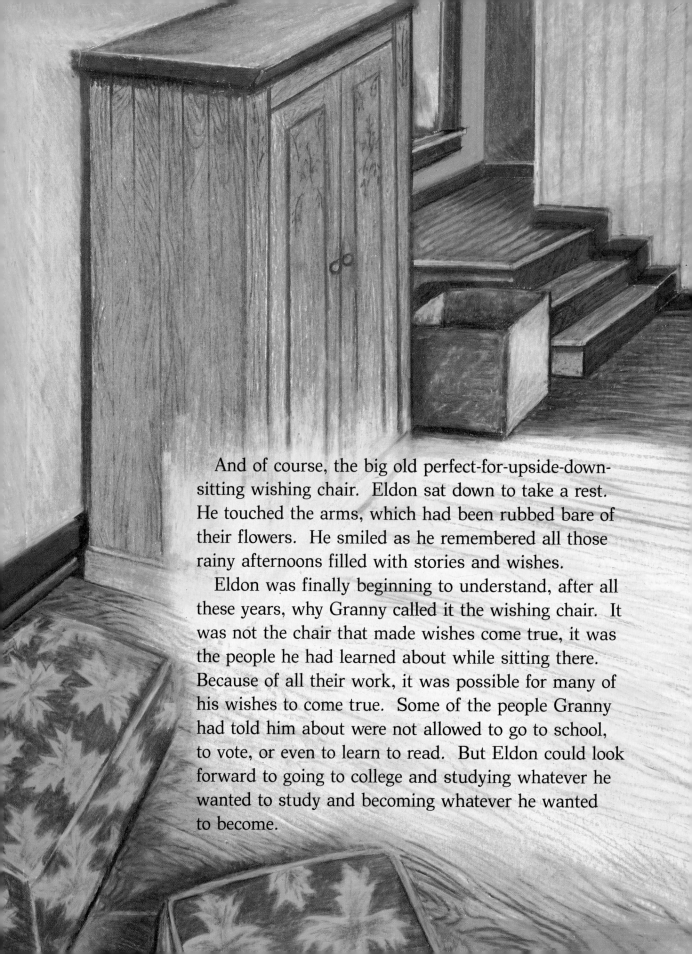

And of course, the big old perfect-for-upside-down-sitting wishing chair. Eldon sat down to take a rest. He touched the arms, which had been rubbed bare of their flowers. He smiled as he remembered all those rainy afternoons filled with stories and wishes.

Eldon was finally beginning to understand, after all these years, why Granny called it the wishing chair. It was not the chair that made wishes come true, it was the people he had learned about while sitting there. Because of all their work, it was possible for many of his wishes to come true. Some of the people Granny had told him about were not allowed to go to school, to vote, or even to learn to read. But Eldon could look forward to going to college and studying whatever he wanted to study and becoming whatever he wanted to become.

When Granny came into the room, Eldon was sitting in the wishing chair, looking a little sad. She gave him a hug with her round, warm-as-a-quilt arms. Then she told him one last story. She said:

I knew a boy named Eldon who was proud and strong. As a child, he spent Sundays exploring a treacherous jungle and captaining a huge ship on a stormy sea. Eldon always managed to find a safe harbor. Not even a lake filled with alligators could keep Eldon down.

As he grew older, Eldon didn't fight make-believe battles anymore. But sometimes he had to fight people who thought they could treat him unfairly because of the color of his skin. They didn't think he deserved the things he wished for. But Eldon worked very hard to make his wishes come true, because he knew that each step he took would make the path a little wider for his brothers and sisters who followed.

"Eldon," Thelma said, giving him a kiss, "that old chair has spent enough time taking up space in my life, and I doubt that I can find room for it in the truck. I'm wondering if you would like to have it."

Eldon nodded happily and thanked her for the special gift. It's hard to find the perfect-for-upside-down-sitting, big-purple-flowered, warm-wintertime, story-listening wishing chair.

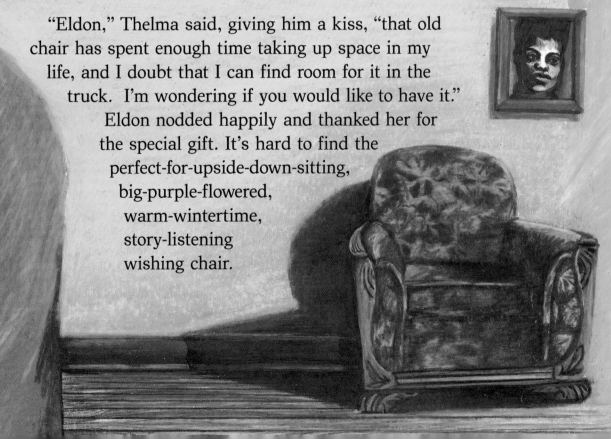

In memory of my brother David, who made me
believe that my wishes could come true.

Library of Congress Cataloging-in-Publication Data

Dupré, Rick.
The wishing chair / by Rick Dupré.
p. cm.
Summary: Eldon comes to know the true power of the wishing
chair at Granny Thelma's as he listens to her stories about the
civil rights workers whose pictures hang above the chair.
ISBN 0-87614-774-0
[1. Civil rights workers—Fiction. 2. Afro-Americans—Fiction.
3. Grandmothers—Fiction. 4. Wishes—Fiction] I. Title.
PZ7.D9284W   1993
[E]—dc20   92-38880
                                                            CIP
                                                             AC

Manufactured in the United States of America

1 2 3 4 5 6 – P/JR – 98 97 96 95 94 93

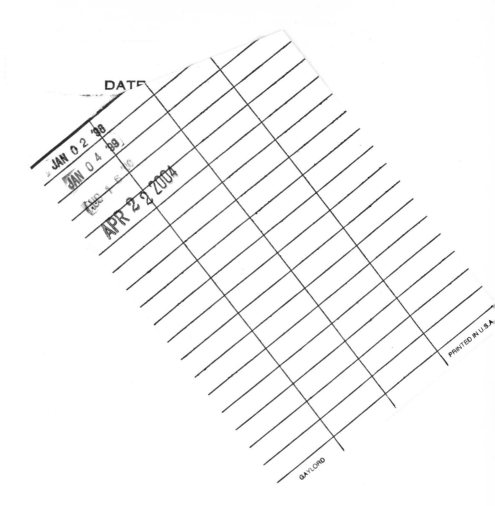

DATE

JAN 0 2 '98

JAN 0 4 '99

APR 2 2 2004

GAYLORD

PRINTED IN U.S.A.